KT-169-087

Usborne
Phonics Readers
Ted in a red bed

Phil Roxbee Cox

Illustrated by Stephen Cartwright

Edited by Jenny Tyler

Language consultant: Marlynne Grant

BSc, CertEd, MEdPsych, PhD, AFBPs, CPsychol

There is a little yellow duck to find on every page.

First published in 2006 by Usborne Publishing Ltd., Usborne House, 83-85 Saffron Hill, London EC1N 8RT, England. www.usborne.com
Copyright © 2006, 1999 Usborne Publishing Ltd.

Ted likes to shop.

Ted stops. Ted hops.
Ted smiles a big smile.

"I like this bed," thinks Ted.

"I like red wood. Red wood is good."

"I want to see more."

"Try the red bed," says Fred.

"Oh, yes," says Ted.

Ted slips his feet under the sheet.

He flops on the pillow.

The pillow is yellow.

"I need this bed, Fred!" grins Ted.

"It is a nice price," smiles Fred.

8

Now it's Ted's bed, not Fred's bed.

Ted feels sleepy.
Ted falls asleep.

Ted has a dream.

He bobs down a stream.

Fred's Beds

Ted has a dream.

He bobs on a wave   into a cave.

11

Ted has a dream.

He can
fly in the sky!

12

Ted has a dream.
He is back by the stream.

Ted wakes up with a snore.

He's not in the store any more.

Ted is home. His bed is home too.

"This red bed must be a magic red bed!"

For Noëlle

First published in 2021 in Great Britain by
Barrington Stoke Ltd
18 Walker Street, Edinburgh, EH3 7LP

www.barringtonstoke.co.uk

This 4u2read edition based on *The Story of Matthew
Buzzington* (Barrington Stoke, 2009)

Text © 2009 & 2021 Andy Stanton
Illustrations © 2009 & 2014 Ross Collins

A CIP catalogue record for this book is available
from the British Library upon request

ISBN: 978-1-80090-046-2

Printed by Hussar Books, Poland

Contents

Chapter 1
Who on Earth Is
Matthew Buzzington?

HELLO, EVERYONE!

And welcome to the Story of Matthew Buzzington.

This story is all about Matthew Buzzington.

It is FULL of Matthew Buzzington.

It is PACKED with Matthew Buzzington.

It is BRIMMING OVER with Matthew Buzzington.

And that is why this story is called ...

The Story of Matthew Buzzington.

But I know what you are saying right now.

You are saying, "Who on Earth is Matthew Buzzington? Is he a pop star with spiky hair and silver trousers?"

No. Matthew Buzzington is not a pop star.

You are saying, "Who on Earth is Matthew Buzzington? Is he a famous footballer who is always on TV scoring goals?"

No. Matthew Buzzington is not a footballer.

You are saying, "Who on Earth is Matthew Buzzington? Is he a secret agent, with a gun in his pocket and a helicopter hidden in his shoe?"

No. Matthew Buzzington is not a secret agent.

"Well, who on EARTH is he then?" you are saying. "Tell me before I go so crazy I eat my own hair!"

Well, there's no need to go crazy or eat your own hair because I will tell you.

In fact, Matthew Buzzington was a normal ten-year-old boy. He had curly brown hair. A friendly face. And three freckles on his left cheek.

Yes, he was just a normal ten-year-old boy.

Except for one thing.

You see, Matthew Buzzington had a special super power.

Matthew Buzzington could turn into a fly.

Just think of that!

A ten-year-old boy turning into a tiny little house fly!

Isn't that amazing?

There was only one problem with Matthew Buzzington's special super power.

It didn't work.

He had spent hours in front of the mirror, trying to turn into a fly.

He had spent days in the park, trying to turn into a fly.

He had spent all of one weekend reading a book called "HOW TO TURN YOURSELF INTO A FLY".

But he still hadn't turned into a fly.

"I KNOW I'm special," Matthew Buzzington told himself every night before he went to sleep. "And one of these days I am going to prove it. One of these days I am going to turn into a fly."

Chapter 2
Off to the Big City

One afternoon Matthew Buzzington was watching TV with his little sister. His little sister's name was Amanda.

Matthew Buzzington and Amanda were lying in front of the TV, looking at a cartoon about a dancing penguin.

"Elephant!" said Amanda. She was only four years old.

"No," said Matthew Buzzington. "No, Amanda. That is a penguin."

"Elephant!" said Amanda.

"No," said Matthew Buzzington again. "Penguin."

"Elephant!" said Amanda.

Just then their parents came into the room.

"Guess what, kids?" said Mum. "We've got something to tell you."

"It's great news," smiled Dad.

Uh oh, thought Matthew Buzzington. You see, he had spotted something.

When grown-ups say they have "great news", it almost always means the news is only great for them. It almost always means trouble for everyone else.

And sure enough it was trouble.

"I've been given a job in the Big City," said Dad. "We will have to move there right away."

"I don't want to move to the Big City!" said Matthew Buzzington. "I want to stay in this nice little town with all my friends!"

"You'll soon make new friends in the Big City," said Mum.

"And my new job means we'll have lots more money," said Dad. "We can buy a swimming pool."

"I don't want a swimming pool," said Matthew Buzzington.

"We can eat in fancy restaurants every night," said Mum.

"I hate fancy restaurants," said Matthew Buzzington. "I can never read the menus because they're always in joined-up writing."

"No more talk," said Dad. "We are leaving for the Big City in two hours, so get packing!"

And his mum and dad went off to pack their bags.

As soon as they had gone from the room, Matthew Buzzington made a sulky face.

"It's not fair," he said. "They are always telling me what to do! But I'm going to teach them a lesson," he said to his little sister, Amanda.

"Elephant!" said Amanda, clapping her hands.

"Yes, I'm going to teach them a lesson," said Matthew Buzzington. "I am going to turn into a fly. Then I am going to fly out of the window. Mum and Dad will look all over, but they will never find me. Then they'll be sorry!"

And so Matthew Buzzington stood there in the middle of the sitting room.

He shut his eyes.

And he said:

"Buzz-buzz-buzz!
My, oh my!
I'm gonna turn myself
Into a fly!"

But nothing happened.

When he opened his eyes again, he was still Matthew Buzzington.

He wasn't a fly at all.

"Matthew!" his mum shouted from the other room. "What's that nonsense about turning into a fly? Stop that and start packing."

*

Two hours later, the whole family were sitting in the car. Mum and Dad were in the front, because that's where the grown-ups go. Matthew Buzzington and Amanda were in the back, because that's where the kids go. They were squashed in with all the bags and cases. It's just not fair, is it?

COUGH-COUGH-SPLUT!

Dad started up the car. Soon they were driving on the busy motorway, driving away from the little town. The Buzzington family was on its way to the Big City.

"What an adventure!" said Mum.

"My new job will make us rich," said Dad.

"Elephant!" said Amanda, who was half asleep.

Matthew Buzzington looked out of the back window. He saw the little town growing smaller and smaller in the distance. In the end he couldn't see it at all.

"I liked our little house in our little town," said Matthew Buzzington. "This is the worst day of my whole life."

Chapter 3
Pineapple Johnson

Matthew Buzzington hated life in the Big City.

He hated the noise of the cars outside his bedroom window. How could anyone sleep at night with so much noise? It was like trying to sleep inside a machine.

He hated the crowds of people everywhere. The people were so mean. They bumped and thumped into him on the street. And they looked right through him as if he wasn't even there.

He hated how there were hardly any trees. In Matthew Buzzington's old town there were lots of trees. But in the Big City there was only one tree. And even that was made out of concrete. And there was bird mess and rude drawings all over it.

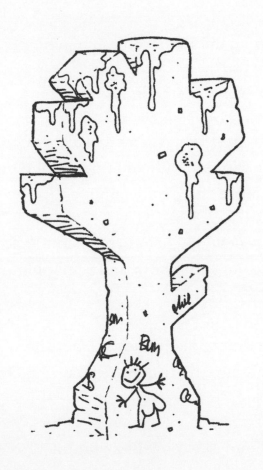

Yes, Matthew Buzzington hated lots of things about the Big City.

But out of all the things he hated, there was one thing he hated most of all.

It was his new school.

And why did he hate it so much?

Because of Pineapple Johnson.

On his first day at the new school, a big, mean-looking kid came up to Matthew Buzzington in the playground.

"Hello, new boy," said the mean-looking kid. He had really short hair and really big muscles in his arms.

"I am Pineapple Johnson," said the mean-looking kid. "Do you know why they call me that?"

"No," said Matthew Buzzington.

"It is because I once threw a pineapple at a teacher," said Pineapple Johnson. "And do you know where that teacher is now?"

"No," said Matthew Buzzington again.

"He is in the hospital," said Pineapple Johnson. "I threw the pineapple so hard that it broke his nose."

"Oh dear," said Matthew Buzzington.

"What can you do to impress me, new boy?" said Pineapple Johnson suddenly.

"What do you mean?" asked Matthew Buzzington.

"Everyone who comes to this school must do something to impress me," said Pineapple Johnson. "If you can impress me, then I will leave you alone for ever. Can you sing?" said Pineapple Johnson.

"No," said Matthew Buzzington. "I am rubbish at singing."

"Do you know any good jokes?" said Pineapple Johnson.

"No," said Matthew Buzzington. "I can never remember jokes."

"Well, what can you do?" said Pineapple Johnson.

"I can turn into a fly," said Matthew Buzzington. "Will that impress you?"

"Yes, it will," said Pineapple Johnson, and he stood very close to Matthew Buzzington with a big mean smile on his big mean face. "If you really can turn into a fly, then I will leave you alone for ever. But if you are lying to me, I will make your life horrible. I will tease you and make fun of you every day."

And he grinned at Matthew Buzzington, but it wasn't a very nice grin. It was the sort of grin a shark might give a goldfish.

So Matthew Buzzington stood there in the playground with everyone watching.

He closed his eyes.

And he said:

"Buzz-buzz-buzz!
My, oh my!
I'm gonna turn myself
Into a fly!"

But nothing happened.

When he opened his eyes again, he was still Matthew Buzzington.

He wasn't a fly at all.

"Sad," said Pineapple Johnson. "What is your name, new boy?"

"Matthew Buzzington," said Matthew Buzzington.

He could feel all the other kids watching him.

He could hear them all whispering.

The other kids were scared of Pineapple Johnson.

They knew Matthew Buzzington was in for a bad time.

"Well, Matthew Buzzington," said Pineapple Johnson. "I am going to make your life horrible, just like I said."

And then Pineapple Johnson took something out from the pocket of his leather jacket.

"See this?" he said. "This is a pineapple seed."

Pineapple Johnson planted the pineapple seed right in the middle of the playground.

"Every day, this seed will grow a little bit bigger," said Pineapple Johnson. "It will grow into a pineapple. A great big one with spikes all over it. And when it is grown I will pull it out of the ground," said Pineapple Johnson. "And I will throw it at your head as hard as I can, Matthew Buzzington. And then – SPLAT! – you will have to go to hospital. Ha ha ha!"

And that is why, out of all the things in the Big City, Matthew Buzzington hated Pineapple Johnson most of all.

Chapter 4
Teasing

Have you ever been teased? It is not a nice feeling. In fact, it is just about the worst feeling in the world.

Being teased gives you a horrible feeling in your tummy. It is such a heavy feeling. It feels like someone has put a bowling ball inside your tummy.

If you are being teased, you walk around with your head down low. You pretend you are looking for something you dropped on the ground. But really you are just hoping that people will forget about you and stop teasing you all the time.

That is what it was like for Matthew Buzzington in his new school. Every day Pineapple Johnson teased him. It was awful.

He called Matthew Buzzington horrible names. He made buzzing sounds like a fly whenever Matthew Buzzington walked by. He said things so mean that Matthew Buzzington wanted to hide away in a deep dark hole.

"Look, it's Buzz-Buzz Buzzington!" said Pineapple Johnson every morning at the start of school. "He thinks he's a fly!"

"Hey, Buzz-Buzz!" said Pineapple Johnson when they were doing P.E. "Why are you climbing up the climbing frame? Why don't you just FLY up instead?"

"Why are you eating that hamburger?" said Pineapple Johnson at lunch time. "Wouldn't you rather eat dog poo, like a real fly? Ha ha ha!"

"Loser!"

"Fly Boy!"

"Insect Face!"

Pineapple Johnson teased Matthew
Buzzington every day.

Matthew Buzzington HATED being teased. He felt like someone had put a bowling ball inside his tummy. He walked around with his head down low. He hoped everyone would forget about him, but they never did. He wished the teachers would see what was going on and stop the teasing. But they were all too busy.

Sometimes, when no one was looking, a tear would drop from Matthew Buzzington's eye and splash on his trainers. After a few weeks, his trainers were the saddest trainers you have ever seen.

"I hate it here in the Big City," said Matthew Buzzington one night as he lay in his bunk bed.

Outside his window the traffic was louder than ever. The cars were VROOOMING along. They sounded a bit like giant flies, buzzing, buzzing, buzzing through the dark night air.

"Elephant!" said Amanda from the bottom bunk.

"I really thought that I could turn into a fly," said Matthew Buzzington as he lay there in his bunk bed. "I thought that I was special. But now I just don't know."

Amanda climbed up the bunk bed and stroked her brother's hair.

"Elephant!" she said softly.

"Thanks, Amanda, but it's no good," said Matthew Buzzington with a sigh.

He turned out the light. And he went to sleep. And he had a dream.

In his dream, Matthew Buzzington was just about to turn into a fly.

"I'm really going to do it this time!" he said. "I'm really going to turn into a fly!"

But just before he could turn into a fly, a great big spiky pineapple came flying out of nowhere.

"NO!" cried Matthew Buzzington in his dream.

SPLAT! went the pineapple as it hit his head.

"Ha ha ha!" laughed the voice of Pineapple Johnson. "You will never turn into a fly! You aren't special, Matthew Buzzington! You aren't special AT ALL!"

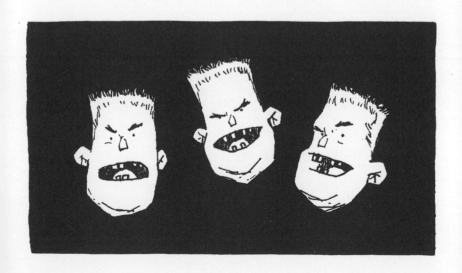

Chapter 5
Matthew Buzzington Gets Into Trouble

It was a rainy Friday afternoon near the end of term. Everyone was fed up.

The kids were fed up of learning.

The teachers were fed up of teaching.

Fat Lenny, the school hamster, was fed up of chewing little bits of paper and straw.

Everyone was fed up.

The clock ticked slowly.

TICK ...

TOCK ...

TICK ...

TOCK ...

Every minute seemed to last an hour. Would it ever be home time?

Outside, the rain poured down. It beat against the windows. It watered the big spiky pineapple growing in the playground.

Pineapple Johnson sat at the back of the class. Pineapple Johnson always sat at the back of the class. It was the best place to sit because the teacher couldn't see what he was up to.

What was Pineapple Johnson up to?

He was drawing something on a scrap of paper. He was laughing as he drew it.

"Ha ha ha!" laughed Pineapple Johnson.

He finished his drawing and passed it to the kid next to him.

The kid next to him giggled and passed it on to the next kid. She giggled too. Then the next kid. Then the next. Then the next.

Last of all, someone passed the scrap of paper to Matthew Buzzington.

Matthew Buzzington looked at the scrap of paper. He saw the drawing that Pineapple Johnson had done. It was a mean cartoon.

The cartoon showed a little fly.

The fly had the face of Matthew Buzzington.

The fly was sitting on a dog poo.

"Mmm, yummy," the Matthew Buzzington fly was saying. "Dog poo is my favourite food in the whole world!"

When Matthew Buzzington saw that cartoon, something snapped inside of him. He was fed up of being teased. He was fed up of Pineapple Johnson. He was fed up of it all.

"I'm fed up of you, Pineapple Johnson!" shouted Matthew Buzzington. "Watch this! I am going to prove that I really CAN turn into a fly once and for all!"

Matthew Buzzington stood up. He stood there in the classroom.

No one dared breathe. They were all watching to see what would happen.

Matthew Buzzington closed his eyes.

And he said:

"Buzz-buzz-buzz!
My, oh my!
I'm gonna turn myself
Into a fly!"

This is it! thought Matthew Buzzington. *I can feel it! At last I'm finally going to turn into a fly!*

He could feel his face change. It was going all hairy.

He could feel little wings growing on his back.

He was sure of it!

But no.

It was all in his mind.

When he opened his eyes again, he was still Matthew Buzzington.

He wasn't a fly at all.

And all the kids were laughing at him.

One kid laughed so hard that a little bit of her sandwich from lunch came back up.

"What's all this mucking around?" demanded the teacher. "I will not have any mucking around in my classroom!"

The teacher grabbed the scrap of paper with the cartoon on.

"Who did this?" she yelled.

"It was Pineapple Johnson!" said Matthew Buzzington. "He's always teasing me!"

"Pineapple Johnson!" said the teacher. "Come and see me in my office after school. I will punish you then."

Then the teacher turned to Matthew Buzzington.

"You come and see me after school as well," she said.

"But why me?" said Matthew Buzzington.

"Because you tell fibs, Matthew Buzzington," said the teacher. "You say you can turn into a fly but you can't. You must stop telling silly fibs. I need to talk to you after school. Now sit back in your chair. I don't want to hear another word from you for the rest of the lesson."

As Matthew Buzzington went to sit down, he saw that Pineapple Johnson was looking hard at him.

Pineapple Johnson looked meaner than ever.

"You got me into this mess," whispered Pineapple Johnson, "but never mind. I've got just the thing for you."

Pineapple Johnson pointed out the window to the pineapple growing in the playground.

"My pineapple is nearly ready," said Pineapple Johnson. "And soon it's going to be coming right for your head. And then – SPLAT! – you will be in the hospital."

"Ha ha ha," laughed Pineapple Johnson.

"Gulp gulp gulp," gulped Matthew Buzzington.

Chapter 6
Locked In!

After school that day, Matthew Buzzington went to the teacher's office. He had never been in trouble with the teacher before. But now he was in deep trouble. And so was Pineapple Johnson.

Pineapple Johnson was already there. He was sitting on a chair outside the teacher's office, waiting for the teacher to call them inside.

"Well, well, well," said Pineapple Johnson. "It's Buzz-Buzz Buzzington. Seen any hungry spiders lately?" he laughed.

"I am fed up of you," said Matthew Buzzington bravely. "I am fed up of how mean you are. And besides—"

"Elephant!" came a voice just then.

"Eh?" said Pineapple Johnson. "What on Earth are you talking about, you weirdo?"

"It wasn't me," said Matthew Buzzington. "I'm not the one who said 'Elephant!'"

He looked down the corridor and saw his little sister, Amanda.

"What are you doing here, Amanda?" said Matthew Buzzington. "You should be back home by now."

"Elephant!" said Amanda.

"What a pair of weirdos," laughed Pineapple Johnson, making a rude face. "One of you thinks he can turn into a fly and one of you can only say 'Elephant!'"

"Elephant!" said Amanda happily.

At that moment the clock on the wall struck four o'clock with a BING! sound that made them all jump.

BING!

BING!

BING!

BING!

"That's odd," said Matthew Buzzington. "Where is the teacher? School finished half an hour ago. The teacher should be here by now."

It was true. The teacher was nowhere to be seen. But do you know what? The teacher had forgotten all about Matthew Buzzington and

Pineapple Johnson. The teacher had gone home to eat her tea and watch a TV quiz show where you could win a million yogurts. The quiz show was called *Who Wants To Win A Million Yogurts?*

Yes, the teacher had gone home. And now it was starting to get dark outside.

"We'd better go home before the caretaker locks the front door," said Matthew Buzzington.

But just then he heard a terrible sound. It was the sound of a big brass key turning in a big brass lock. The caretaker was locking the front door.

"Quick!" shouted Matthew Buzzington. "We've got to let the caretaker know we're locked in the school!"

Pineapple Johnson, Matthew Buzzington and Amanda ran down the corridor towards the front door. But they were too late. By the time they got to the door, the caretaker had vanished. He had gone home to watch *Who Wants To Win A Million Yogurts?*

"There must be another way out," said Pineapple Johnson. "The school has lots of doors and windows."

But all the doors they tried were locked. And all the windows too. Every single one.

"We're trapped in the school!" said Matthew Buzzington.

Suddenly, just to make things worse, all the lights went out. It was pitch-black inside the school.

"Waaah!" cried a voice in the darkness. "Waaaaaaaah!"

Matthew Buzzington thought that the crying was coming from Amanda. He turned around.

"There, there," said Matthew Buzzington kindly. "It's OK, Amanda."

But Amanda was fine. She wasn't crying at all. She was playing with some fluff she'd found. The crying was coming from Pineapple Johnson.

"Waaaah!" sobbed Pineapple Johnson. "I don't like it, I'm scared!"

"You? Scared?" said Matthew Buzzington. "But you're so tough. You're the toughest boy in the school!"

"But I don't like the dark," sobbed Pineapple Johnson. "And I don't like being away from my mummy. Waaah! Mummy! Mummy!"

"Don't worry, Pineapple," said Matthew Buzzington. He reached out his hand in the darkness and gave Pineapple Johnson a pat on the back. "We'll be all right. And after all—"

But just then the children heard the sound of a window being smashed.

"Climb in," whispered a man's voice.

"Quick, before anyone sees us!"

"You sure this place is empty?" said another voice.

"Yeah, of course it's empty," said the first voice. "And it's a huge school. There'll be plenty of stuff to nick in here."

"Oh, no," said Matthew Buzzington. "Robbers! Robbers have broken into the school!"

Chapter 7
Big Robber and Little Robber

CLOMP!

CLOMP!

CLOMP!

The robbers' heavy steps rang out through the dark school.

"Waaah! Mummy!" sniffed Pineapple Johnson.

"Shut up!" said Matthew Buzzington. "We've got to hide."

But there was nowhere to hide. They were trapped at the end of the long corridor.

CLOMP!

CLOMP!

BASH!

"Ouch!" yelled a voice in pain. "I just bashed my shin on something!"

"Well, turn on your torch, stupid!" said another voice.

The robber turned on his torch.

And now the children could see the robbers walking down the corridor towards them.

Oh, they really looked like robbers!

They had broken noses and scars all over their faces.

One of them was big and fat. He was wearing a jumper which said "Big Robber".

The other robber was small and thin. He was wearing a jumper which said "Little Robber".

"Hang on a moment," said Big Robber. "Where's Medium-Size Robber? Why isn't he helping us rob the school?"

"Medium-Size Robber couldn't make it tonight," said Little Robber. "He's got an important table-tennis match this evening."

"What? Again?" said Big Robber. "Medium-Size Robber's always playing table tennis! I'm sick of it!"

"Hang on," whispered Little Robber. "What's this?"

Little Robber shone his torch right into the far corner of the corridor.

"HEY!" he yelled. "It's a bunch of kids! What you doing here?" he growled. "Are you spying on us? Is that what you're up to?"

"N-n-no," said Matthew Buzzington as he shook with fright. "W-w-we just got locked in by mistake, that's all. We weren't s-s-spying, I p-promise!"

"What are your names, kids?" said Big Robber.

"Matthew Buzzington," said Matthew Buzzington.

"Elephant!" said Amanda.

"Mummy!" said Pineapple Johnson.

"Funny names for kids," said Big Robber, and scratched his head.

"Never mind that now!" said Little Robber. "What we gonna do with 'em?"

"What do you think we're gonna do with 'em? We're gonna lock 'em up so we can get on with robbing stuff, of course," said Big Robber.

Big Robber flashed his torch on the big wooden door at the end of the corridor.

"GYM" said a sign on the door.

"Perfect!" said the robbers together. They pushed the children into the gym.

Then:

SLAM!

LOCK!

That was that.

The kids were locked inside the dark gym.

Chapter 8
You Can Do It,
Matthew Buzzington!

It was cold inside the gym. And it smelled of damp socks and stinky feet.

The kids could hear the robbers outside, as they smashed down doors, looking for stuff to steal.

"Look what I found! A brand-new computer!" they heard Little Robber say.

"Brilliant! Put it in the bag," said Big Robber. "We'll soon be rich! And I'm not sharing ANY of it with Medium-Size Robber!"

Back in the gym, Matthew Buzzington was shaking his head.

"It's not fair," said Matthew Buzzington. "It's just not fair at all! If only there was some way out of here."

But there were no windows in the gym. And the robbers had locked the door.

"There's only one thing for it," said Matthew Buzzington. "My chance has come at last!"

"What do you mean?" said Pineapple Johnson.

"I'll have to turn into a fly," said Matthew Buzzington. "Then I will fly through the keyhole. Once I am on the other side of the door, I will unlock it and we can all escape."

"OK," said Pineapple Johnson. "That sounds like a good plan."

"What?" said Matthew Buzzington. "You're not going to make fun of me and call me Buzz-Buzz Buzzington?"

"No," said Pineapple Johnson. "You've been really nice to me tonight. I'm sorry for all the times I teased you. If you say you can turn into a fly, I believe you can."

"Thank you," said Matthew Buzzington. "You're the very first person to ever believe I can turn into a fly."

Matthew Buzzington stood in the middle of the gym. And he closed his eyes. And he thought about it really hard.

Not just really hard, but REALLY hard.

Not just REALLY hard, but REALLY REALLY hard.

Not just REALLY REALLY hard, but REALLY REALLY REALLY REALLY REALLY REALLY REALLY

REALLY REALLY REALLY REALLY REALLY REALLY REALLY REALLY REALLY hard.

He said:

"Buzz-buzz-buzz!
My, oh my!
I'm gonna turn myself
Into a fly!"

And guess what?

There was a flash of green light.

There was a little popping noise, like a cork popping out of a bottle.

And suddenly Pineapple Johnson and Amanda saw Matthew Buzzington vanish.

In his place was a tiny little fly.

Matthew Buzzington had done it at last!

Chapter 9
The Battle of the Playground

WHEEEEEEEEEEEEEEEE!

The little fly did a loop-the-loop and went buzzing all over the gym in joy. Then, quick as a flash, it zoomed over to the keyhole and squeezed through.

As soon as it was outside, the fly turned back into Matthew Buzzington. Matthew Buzzington unlocked the door. He was just about to fling it open when the robbers ran round the corner, flashing their torches.

"OI!" shouted Big Robber.

"How did you escape?" shouted Little Robber.

"Uh oh!" said Matthew Buzzington.

"Buzz-buzz-buzz!
My, oh my!
I'm gonna turn myself
Into a fly!"

Now he'd got the hang of it, it was easy.

There was another green flash and another little popping noise. And suddenly Matthew Buzzington was a fly again.

"Huh? Where did he go?" said Big Robber.

"He turned himself into a fly!" said Little Robber in amazement. "After him!"

Together the robbers chased the fly down the corridor, yelling and shouting as they ran. The fly looped and buzzed and flew around like mad. But the robbers were fast.

Big Robber took out a newspaper from his back pocket. He rolled it up.

SMACK!

Big Robber smacked the fly with the newspaper.

The fly tried to dodge, but the newspaper smashed its wings. The fly's wings crumpled up.

"BZZZZZZ!" said the fly. It flopped out of a broken window and landed in the playground. The robbers climbed out after it.

"Now we've got him!" they laughed.

"Bzzz bzzzz bzzz," said the Matthew Buzzington fly. It tried to fly away, but it was no good. Its wings were all crumpled. The fly tried to turn back into a boy, but that didn't work either. It was too weak.

All it could do was crawl along the playground through the rain and the puddles.

"Bzz bzz," said the Matthew Buzzington fly.

It could hear the robbers' voices high above, booming and loud.

"Squash him, Little Robber," said Big Robber.

And then the Matthew Buzzington fly saw a big, dirty boot coming down from above.

The boot came closer ...

"Ha ha," laughed Little Robber. "It's all over for you, my tiny friend!"

The boot came closer ...

Closer ...

Closer ...

But just as the boot was about to crush the fly, something came whooshing through the dark night air.

WHOOOOOOOOOOOOOOOOOOOSSSSSHHHHH!

It was an enormous pineapple!

SPLAT!

The pineapple hit Little Robber right on the nose and knocked him right out.

"Got him!" cried Pineapple Johnson. He had got out of the gym after Matthew Buzzington unlocked the door. "That was my best throw ever!"

But then the fly looked up.

Uh-oh.

"You may have knocked out Little Robber, but I'm still here!" said Big Robber.

Big Robber lifted up his newspaper and held it over the fly.

"What you gonna do now?" Big Robber laughed. "Your friend ain't got no more pineapples. And now I'm gonna squash you once and for all, you stupid little fly!"

Chapter 10
Elephant!

Big Robber's newspaper came closer.

"Say your prayers," laughed Big Robber. "You're about to die ..."

TRUMPET!

"Eh?" said the robber, looking around in fear. "What on Earth was that?"

TRUMPET!

And suddenly an enormous elephant came around the corner, swinging its long trunk.

TRUMPET!

It galloped towards Big Robber.

"Aaaarrgggh!" shouted Big Robber.

He went running off down the playground.
But a big elephant can catch a mean robber
any day.

TRUMPET!

The elephant caught up with Big Robber in
no time flat.

"AAAAARRRGGGH!"

The last thing that Big Robber saw was the
elephant's bottom coming towards him in the
rainy night.

SQUASH!

Big Robber was squashed into the
playground by two-and-a-half tons of big fat
elephant.

"What on Earth was that?" said Pineapple
Johnson.

"I don't believe it," said Matthew Buzzington. At last he had finally turned himself back into a boy. "Is that elephant who I think it is?"

As they watched, there was a puff of pink smoke and a very loud popping sound.

The enormous animal was gone.

And sitting there in its place was four-year-old Amanda Buzzington.

"Elephant!" she said. "Elephant!"

"That's right!" laughed Matthew Buzzington, running over to Amanda.

He picked her up in his arms and gave her a great big hug. "Elephant! Clever girl, Amanda! Clever girl!"

Chapter 11
Matthew Buzzington Is Happy

After that, it was easy. The children climbed over the school gate and asked someone to ring the police. And the police came and took the robbers away.

"Well done, children," said the police woman as she put handcuffs on the robbers. "But how did three children like you stop these two strong men?"

"Take us away! Take us away! There's superhero insects and magic elephants and flying pineapples!" cried the robbers. "Take us away!"

"What are they talking about?" said the police woman.

"No idea," said Matthew Buzzington with a grin. "I think they must be a bit crazy or something."

And that was the last anyone saw of Big Robber and Little Robber.

Well, from that day on, everything got a lot better in Matthew Buzzington's life.

Pineapple Johnson turned out to be a very nice boy after all.

"I'm sorry I was so mean to you before," he said. "But you see, my family moved to the Big City last year. I didn't have any friends. I was so lonely and sad. I became a bully to hide how unhappy I felt."

"I've been unhappy in the Big City too," said Matthew Buzzington. "I haven't got any friends either. Perhaps you and me can be friends."

"Elephant!" said Amanda.

And do you know what? Matthew Buzzington and Pineapple Johnson did become the best of friends. They spent lots of time together.

They played games together. They watched *Who Wants To Win A Million Yogurts?* on TV together. They even planted pineapples together.

But they didn't throw the pineapples at people. They made them into delicious pineapple milkshakes.

And they let Amanda join in all their games, even though she was much younger than them and only ever said "Elephant!"

So everyone was happy and it all worked out for the best.

And that is the Story of Matthew Buzzington.

So remember – next time you are about to squash a fly, or smack it with a newspaper, or zap it with fly-spray, just think twice.

Because it could be Matthew Buzzington.

And next time you are about to shoot an elephant, or smack it with a cricket bat, or zap it with elephant-spray, just think twice.

It could be Amanda.

And next time you are about to throw a pineapple at someone's head, just think twice.

ONLY EVER throw a pineapple at someone's head if you really have to. Like if that person is a robber or something.

Otherwise, the best thing is to make a nice pineapple milkshake and share it with your friends.

Wouldn't you agree?